KU-783-458

The EaTiNG MONSTeR

with the see-through tummy

Written & illustrated by
Valentina Mendicino

IMAGINE THAT™

Licensed exclusively to Imagine That Publishing Ltd
Tide Mill Way, Woodbridge, Suffolk, IP12 1AP, UK
www.imaginethat.com
Copyright © 2015 Valentina Mendicino
All rights reserved
0 2 4 6 8 9 7 5 3 1
Manufactured in China

Written and illustrated by Valentina Mendicino

All rights reserved. No part of this publication may be reproduced, stored in a retrieval system, or
transmitted in any form or by any means, electronic, mechanical, photocopying, recording or otherwise,
without the prior written permission of the publisher. Neither this book nor any part or any of the
illustrations, photographs or reproductions contained in it shall be sold or disposed of otherwise than as
a complete book, and any unauthorised sale of such part illustration, photograph or reproduction shall be
deemed to be a breach of the publisher's copyright.

ISBN 978-1-78445-538-5

A catalogue record for this book is available from the British Library

This is the Eating Monster.

He's not very good at reading ...

... or doing sports!

In fact, the only thing
the Eating Monster really loves to do is ...

One day, the Eating Monster decided to try eating new things.

This got him into BIG trouble with his neighbours!

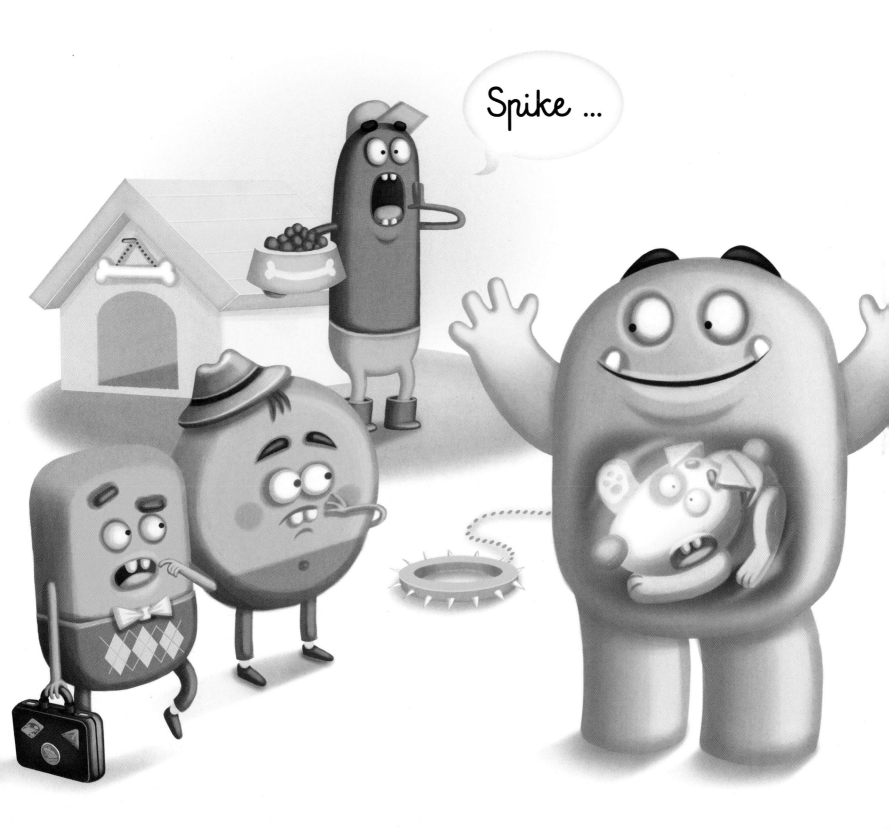

The Eating Monster was ALWAYS hungry and the more he ate ...

... the BIGGER he got!

The Eating Monster ate so much and grew so big that ...

He couldn't sleep in his bed any more.

He couldn't tie his shoelaces.

Oops ...

He couldn't sit at his school desk.

He couldn't play hide-and-seek.

One, two, three ...

He couldn't ride his bike.

In fact, the Eating Monster grew so big, he couldn't even fit through his front door any more!

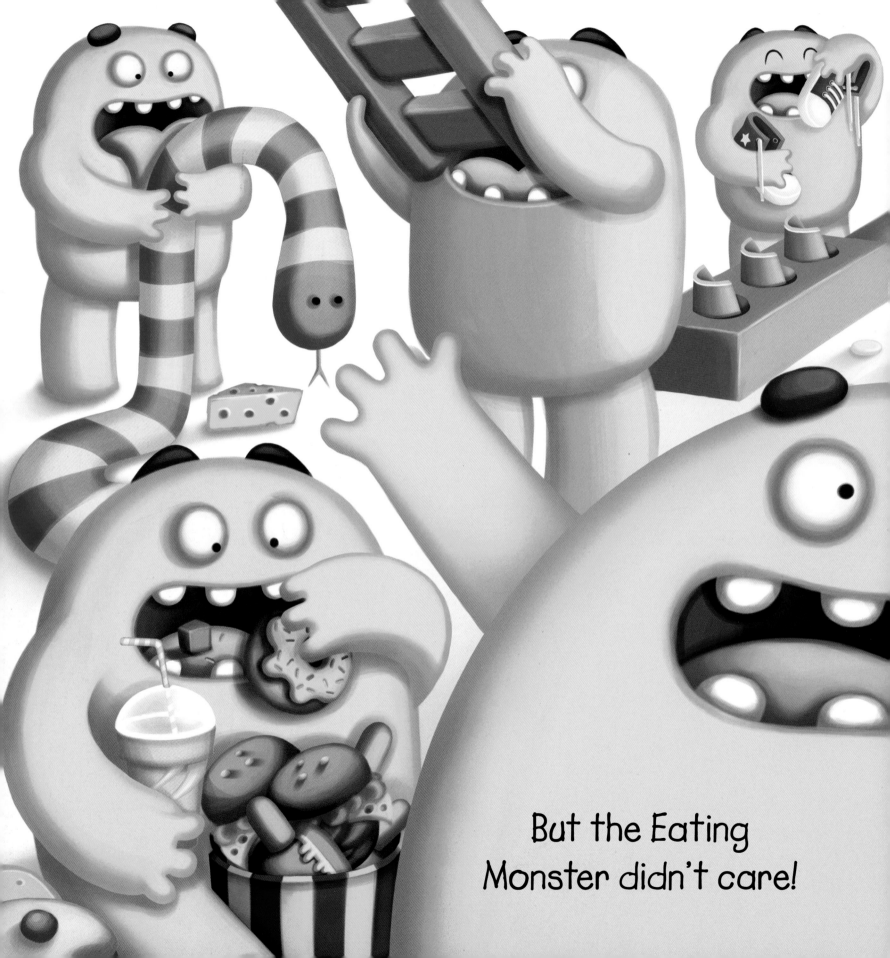

But the Eating Monster didn't care!

He just wanted to eat and taste EVERYTHING!

So the Eating Monster got ...

... AND BIGGER ...

... AND BIGGER ...

BIGGER

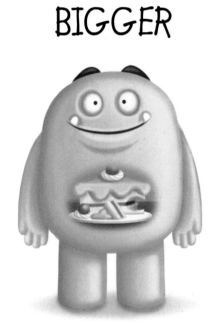

Unfortunately, as the Eating Monster got bigger, so did the things that he wanted to eat!

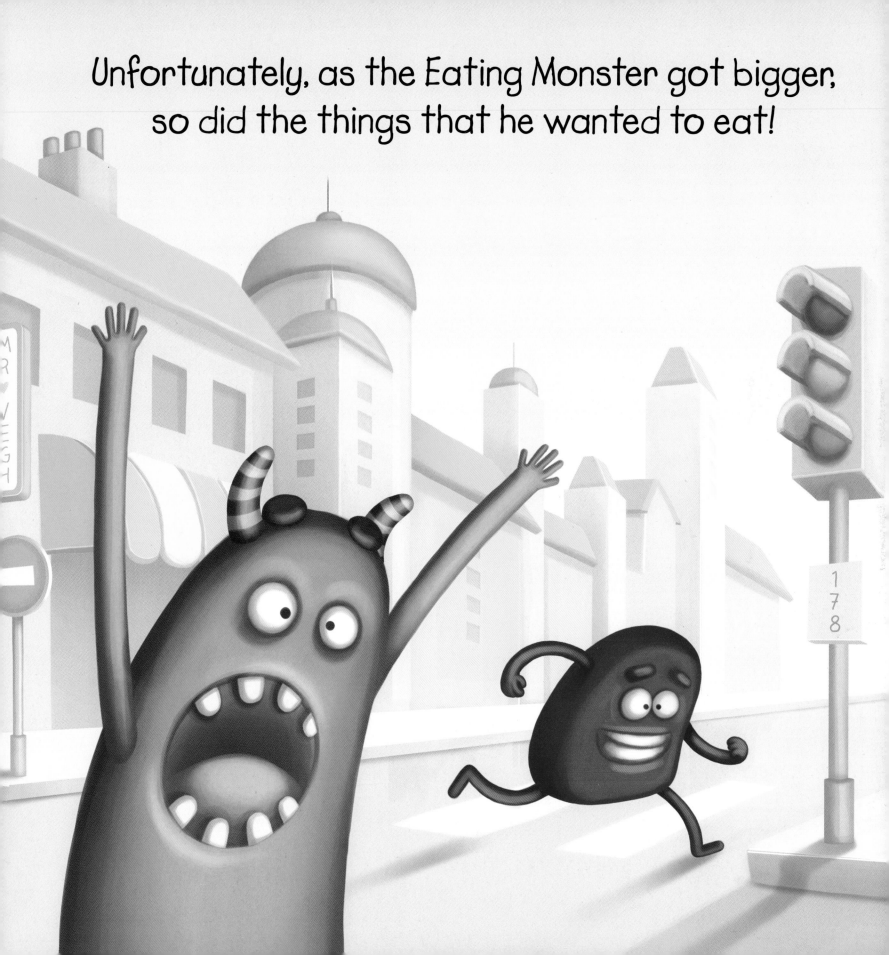

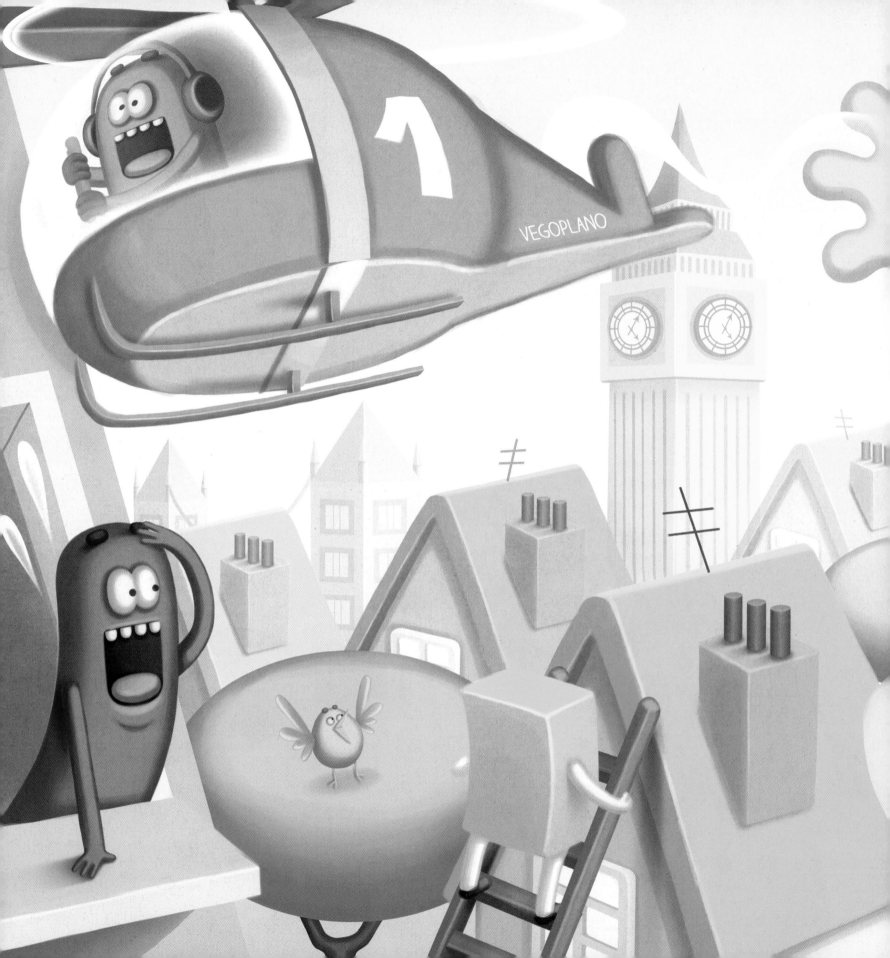

he never
thought that he
would end up ...